BEAUREGARD

of

BALLARAT

A HAPPY TALE

AS TOLD TO

SHAPOOR BATLIWALLA

**RYAN
PUBLISHING**

First published 2020 by Ryan Publishing
PO Box 7680, Melbourne, 3004
Victoria, Australia
Ph: 61 3 9505 6820
Email: books@ryanpub.com
Website: www.ryanpub.com

 A catalogue record for this
book is available from the
National Library of Australia

Title: *Beauregard of Ballarat: A Happy Tale*

Paperback: 9781876498740
Hardback: 9781876498801
eBook: 9781876498689

Internal and cover design by Luke Harris, Working Type Studio,
Victoria, Australia. www.workingtype.com.au

This story is dedicated to all my feathered, furred and four-footed friends who go unheard or unheeded their entire lives.

Our silence is put down to stupidity.

This is my attempt to prove otherwise, to share our thoughts and feelings and to show how our simple ways could improve the lives of those smart enough to listen.

— *Beauregard.*

ABOUT THE AUTHOR

Shapoor Batliwalla was born in Mumbai, India in the 1950s, a halcyon and happy period in Indian history, following the discovery of Penicillin and before the advent of the IPL.

He attended 6 schools in 5 different countries although he is adamant this was more an outcome of his family's nomadic existence than any particular scholastic ineptitude.

His only notable achievement through his entire boyhood appears to be that he once bowled 6 balls to Sir Geoff Boycott at the Royal Bangkok Sports Club cricket nets before being advised to take up Scrabble instead.

In his 20s, Mr Batliwalla moved to Australia and loathing real work of any sort, turned to Australian TV and Cinema, playing a string of doctors, lawyers and assorted head-wobbling sub-continentals; minor character roles hardly substantial enough to satisfy stomach or soul.

In time, as his daughters grew vocal enough to demand regular if not daily feeding, he was compelled to seek more reliable and regular employment.

This he did by joining a leading Melbourne advertising agency as a copywriter. For the next 40 years, he managed to avoid scrutiny or detection by the simple yet long-heralded advertising tradition of going out to an early lunch and staying there.

Eventually discovered hiding under a desk in 2018, he was summarily despatched into the timeless morass of tedium called retirement where he attempted to pass the time by writing, for the first time ever, without the misinformation of a brief, the misguidance of a planner or the misdirections of a client.

Mr Batliwalla lives in Melbourne with his two daughters, two sons-in-law, two mortgages, two dogs, and two cats.

He has however, in perhaps the only wise move of his entire life, limited himself to one wife.

CHAPTER 1

I have always believed that true beauty comes from within and has nothing do with appearance. It's a wonderful philosophy to have when one's mother is a Chihuahua and father a Whippet. People find that hard to envisage but I am living proof that when one finds love, it's no big deal to go find a ladder.

That said, I have to assure you that from what I hear, I am a rather distinguished-looking fellow. When humans meet me for the first time, I hear some very flattering things. Of course, being human, one cannot take what they say at face value, given their fondness for contrivance and concealment, but we dogs have learnt how to interpret their true meaning.

For example, they look at me and say, 'how interesting' which is of course human for 'unique' and another way of acknowledging that I am an original.

Another term I often hear is 'how unusual', which of course everyone knows, is just a euphemism for 'distinctive'. Or perhaps, most flattering of all, 'how amusing', which can only refer to my entertaining personality and keen wit.

Back to my parents. Mother lives in a little house on the west side of historic Ballarat, a regional city in Victoria, Australia, of about 105,000 people, some two hours drive west of Melbourne. It's large enough to give a dog room to roam, and small enough to imbue him with simple rural values.

It was started in 1835 by sheep herders moving to the area and once gold was discovered there in the 1850s it developed rapidly, with elegant colonial buildings, quaint cottages and large green parks, situated around beautiful Lake Wendouree.

The story goes that 'wendouree' means 'go away' in the local aboriginal language. When a well-meaning Scotsman named William Yullie saw an indigenous woman sitting by a swamp, he asked her what it was called. She, quite understandably, told the weirdly accented white fella' to bugger off. Enchanted by this melodic and exotic-sounding name, the lake subsequently built there was named Wendouree, in mistaken tribute to the swamp that had once existed in its place.

Mother looks after a friendly, middle-aged couple named Don and Di Rivers. They dote on mother, even when she is in what we kids would call, her 'Mexican' mood.

Mother has been looking after them since she was a pup, and I must say, they both looked very well for it. Good sturdy confirmation of the limbs. None of the back or hip problems that humans are so prey to. No discernible scurf, fleas or ticks.

Father lived three doors down, caring for an elderly gentleman named Bertie Butler. As mother tells it, dad managed to sneak out of the Butler household one day when Bertie went out for his weekly six pack of Southern Comfort and Cola. He was wandering around the street, enjoying the local lawns and lampposts, when, as mother describes it, he picked up the scent of mother's Eau D'Amour (mother speaks several languages).

He jumped the Rivers' three-foot picket fence, got down on his knees and elbows (never could figure out why mother always smiled when she told us this) and that was it. Magic happened and a few months later, we were born.

Mother tells us that Don and Di were very concerned for her wellbeing, given the disparate size of dam and sire, but when the time came, she talked them through the night, calmed them down with little nudges and nibbles and eventually, discharged her obligations to dad and nature by discharging the three of us.

I came first, then my younger brother and after him, our little sister. I suppose I owe my sober, reliable nature to the fact that being the eldest, I had a responsibility to look after my younger siblings. As much as I hungered for mother's love, I always made sure I left a drop or two for them.

Mother was named Marguerite, a Mexican flower I believe and in the true Aussie tradition of truncation, was called Margie for short.

Dad's name was Bob. Not the most fanciful name in the world but in mother's words, 'as basic and simple as the cur himself'. I guess that was her way of saying it suited him.

Most days dad came round to visit us though it seemed he was more interested in sniffing around mother's food bowl than sniffing us.

As babies, we realised that dad could provide none of the nurturing nectar that mother lavished upon us and got really shirty if we tried to get it out of him. It's not that he was a bad dad, it's just that he seemed to be badly built, with none of the interesting protruding bits that mother comforted us with.

He was however, lean and incredibly athletic. One day, at mother's request, he was babysitting us when a rather rowdy Russian Blue said something rude to him and off he went in pursuit like a torpedo in a tail wind. Mother did say that it was typical of his kind. 'Tell them they're needed and watch them run.' Not sure if that was about Whippets in particular or a more general statement on fatherhood.

We were very fortunate that from a very early age, mother taught us about our roles in life, what was expected of us.

Unlike humans who can spend an entire lifetime trying to discover their purpose on this earth, we dogs are very clear about it.

Our role is to look after the humans placed in our care, as best we can. I don't mean the obvious guarding the house, barking at strangers, watchdog stuff. That's just a basic property service we provide in exchange for a warm bed and an occasional ear rub. No, I'm talking about the careful monitoring of and ministering to the health and wellbeing of our charges.

Mother was very clear about our responsibilities. For example, humans are well known she said, when taken on a walk, to dither and dally, drag their feet, even stop to talk to other humans. This is hardly an effective way to get air into the lungs and keep the blood pumping.

In such cases, it is our responsibility to hurry them along, pulling and straining, thereby raising their aerobic rate and providing them an effective cardiovascular workout.

Similarly if, when wrapped in the arms of daytime TV, they forget it's feeding time, it is our duty to remind them with short sharp barks or a little ankle nip or two. It is how we keep their brains on track, functioning normally and away from the depressing doldrums of dementia. Or most basic of all, just keeping their extremities warm and frostbite free by lying on them in bed. These and a hundred more such acts of care are what dogs are put on this earth for.

One of the first things mother taught was a little mantra we were to practise on our humans when we moved in with them:

> 'When you're down or in a muddle,
> let your dog give you a cuddle.
>
> When you're ill or feeling sick,
> let your dog give you a lick.
>
> When life is a big mishap,
> let your dog onto your lap'.

Sadly, many of you humans will never experience this but I have to tell you, it is very fulfilling to know exactly what one's purpose in life is.

CHAPTER 2

Initially, my siblings and I were happy just to spend time with mother, wrestle among ourselves, keep Don and Di entertained by wriggling about on their laps. But time came when instinctively we knew we were ready to start caring for own human wards, to discover the world, and mark our own lamp posts. Don and Di did not need us, they were supremely well looked after by mother and as mother often said, she did not have us for 'her sake, but for our sakes.'

In other words, it was time to leave the crowded family bed to discover the joys of a one-dog blanket. It was time to adopt our own human wards and make a life of our own.

I don't think humans are as good at 'moving on' as all other living creatures are. They cling to each other, holding on not because, as they often say, they enjoy the closeness but because in reality, they seem to need the security.

I understand you find change scary, but as we see it, change is the catalyst that makes everything happen. It is the impetus to keep exploring and, as you may have noticed when a cold nose starts to probe your crotch, we dogs love to explore. Without a step into the unknown, a new direction, what would we ever discover or achieve?

A human child, cradled and coddled forever, never discovers the joys of independence and adulthood. They just turn into older, less capable children. To be clear, none of us, human or better, ever lose the connection we have with our parents or families.

If, say six months from now, I had the opportunity to visit mother again, I know we'd have a wonderful time, sharing memories, talking about my new life, having a good old laugh. But I have no doubt that after some time, she would say to me, 'OK, vamoose back to where you came from, I have my life to get on with.' With us dogs, bonds are spiritual, not physical. That's how we ease the uncertainty of separation without confining ourselves to a status quo.

Mother explained to us that soon we would have to choose the wards we wanted to take care of. 'People will come by for you to see', she explained. 'Do not hurry into your decision. Take your time, have a good sniff of their ankles and see whether you feel there is a healthy emotional fit between you. If there is, then play with them, rub against their legs. Put your neck and ears where their fingers can tickle you. But if you do not immediately feel that this is right for you, after all, it's a lifetime of commitment, be polite, say hello then come back and stand behind me so they understand that you are saying 'no thank you.' It is crucial that you let your heart rule your head.'

This may surprise some of you humans who have invented so many ruses to avoid listening to your hearts with rationality, logic, intellect, reasoning, sense, sanity and syllogism. You have created entire branches of philosophies dedicated to explaining away your fear of letting your instinct and emotions guide you.
The way we see it, all the meaningful things in life such as love, friendship, loyalty, tolerance, trust, compassion, kindness and charity, all come from the heart.

When we choose a human to spend our lives with, we don't deliberate on things like, 'will they provide for us well' or 'look good on a leash', or 'leave us a fortune when they go.'

We choose our partners simply by the exhilarating rush of joy, the 'whoosh' of wonder, the feeling of instant belonging you feel when you meet that special person.

Please, this may help you understand us a bit better so it's worth knowing. Heads can confuse, deceive and delude you. They give you options, alternatives and arguments. But your heart never will!

Most importantly, we learnt a long time ago that emotional attachment is the only bond strong enough to survive the thousand disappointments one will experience in a long relationship. It is only the strength of one's emotional connections that make possible the many compromises that mutual contentment demands you make.

Logic is fine when everything is going well but only the depth of your feelings can help you survive the tough times.

After all, if anything can salvage a rocky relationship it's forgiveness and that's a quality that can only come from the heart. That is why, whatever you do, your dog will never think of throwing in the towel or filing for a dogvorce. He or she will just continue caring.

Hopefully one day, you humans will put all your rationalising aside and evolve to this higher level of allowing your heart to override all the confusion a head can conjure up.

That day, you will find yourselves as happy as a dog.

*Father and Mother. Proof that nothing brings
a man to his knees faster than love.*

CHAPTER 3

Mother was right. People were soon brought before us and as she said, the choice became easy when we let our feelings take over.

The first humans that came were a young couple with a little girl of their own. I liked them, but felt that I could not entirely deliver to them the constant, mindless playfulness that would be required to keep the little girl happy.

I have always been a bit of a thinker and knew I would be better suited to a human who needed my philosophic guidance and well-considered counselling. So, I retreated back to our bed, as did my brother.

My sister though, being the playful, happy sort of child that she was, hit it off instantly with the little girl. She squeaked and rolled in delight as the little girl squealed and stroked her. They were both clearly happier for having found one another and soon, wishing us goodbye, my sister excitedly led her new humans out the door. Mother was elated. Pleased, she said, because my sister was getting a good family and also because she, mother, was that much closer to getting her figure back.

The very next day, a man walked in with his son, a pug ugly boy of about 12 with red hair, freckles, chubby arms and obviously a very physical sort of boy. Brother always loved a bit of rough housing, always up for a wrestle and tireless in trying to pin me down. The boy and he were obviously a match made in heaven, wriggling and writhing about as the boy tried to roll brother onto his back and brother tried to bring the boy down by eating his shoe laces.

'Yeah, he's grouse', the boy said to his father and soon, I was the only one left with mother.

For the next few days, no one came for me to evaluate until one morning, the door bell rang and I heard voices in the hallway. Shortly after the door to the laundry, our designated domicile, opened and there stood Di with a lady who simply exuded goodness. The moment I looked up at her, my heart started to sing. Obviously, I had to go sniff things out more thoroughly.

Many humans think that we dogs use our noses simply to identify people. Very wrong. We use our noses to categorise people. You see, we can smell more than just a scent or an aroma. Through our noses we can actually smell your personality traits.

For example, angry, hostile people often exude an acrid, burning sort of smell. Unhappy or pessimistic people smell of old socks, rotting rubber or mouldy cheese. Happy, optimistic people smell of sunlight and soap. Unkind or cruel people smell of smoke, sweat and stale beer.

This lady smelled of talcum powder, lavender and lily of the valley. My nose told me she was kindness personified. 'What a lovely little fellow', she said to Di, then after a pause, 'he looks so....soulful.'

At last! Someone who could see the thinker in me, the scholar, the sophist. My human had arrived!

Soulful was spot on. That's what I am. You see, I'm not one for chasing balls. I am a chaser of concepts, ideologies and beautiful thoughts. Instinctively, my tail started to move from side to side as I tried to signal to mother that 'this one needs me.'

She had silvery white hair, like a great fluffy cloud, surrounding a round, cheerful face. Rosy pink cheeks and the clearest blue eyes. The smile and laugh lines under her eyes told me that she was someone who always saw the bright side of things. She walked with a stick, being a little stooped and what mother called, a 'little past her best days'.

Who cared?

She smelled of gentle pats and freshly baked dog biscuits. Of cuddles by a fireside and soft woollen blankets. She looked generous and genial and grandmotherly. Yet, and this is what absolutely convinced me that her place henceforth was by my side, was that she also smelled just a little lonely.

Di, as anxious as mother was to return to being a one dog house asked her a bit nervously, 'What do you think Irene?'

Irene! What a charming, gentle, serene name. She

looked down at me, then with a little effort bent down and tickled me in a spot behind my ear no one had ever discovered before. I think I actually quivered a bit. This woman had everything I was looking for in a human.

She stood up, looked at Di and said, 'I think he's lovely.'

Oh, how my heart beat. Lovely! I'd never been called that.

Don called me 'champ' and Di called me 'squirt' and mother often called me 'you greedy little nibbler' but 'Lovely?' That wonderful word that said sweet and loveable and gorgeous and cuddly all at the same time.

My tail wagged even faster. I was trying to tell mother that I would have this one. Irene saw it and laughed out loud.

'Oh the little darling. Look! He has such a happy little tail!'

I walked out of mother's house that morning happy and proud. I'd got the pick of the people.

CHAPTER 4

Our house, the one that Irene and I would share, was not grand or fancy, but I thought it perfect. It was warm and cosy with a bedroom, living area, and kitchen with a small dinner table. A bathroom out the back and a small room off to one side that Irene called the 'spare' room. The house was long and a little dark, an old solid stone cottage built sometime towards the end of Ballarat's gold mining boom, Irene told me.

It had a tiny frontage with a bright blue front door that led you into a long hallway. At first, I thought it smelled a bit damp but no problem, I'd soon have that wonderful musty, homely, doggy smell running through it. Out the back was a small but perfectly maintained yard with enough lawn for me to squat on and joy of joy, a dog's favourite convenience, a large lemon tree.

I ran about the place gleefully. It had everything I could

possibly want. A thick, shaggy carpet, a gas fire, a comfortable, beaten-up couch and best of all, placed in a corner of the living room by the fire, a brand new bed for me. It was thick and soft and the moment I got in, I knew that once I fixed the place up a bit, a few hairs, a couple of shredded socks or bits of fluffy slipper, it would be ideal.

People tend to judge an abode by its size, cost and opulence while we dogs judge it simply by the warmth within. Your way is devised to help you find an impressive house. Ours is designed to help us find a happy home.

I climbed into my new bed, turned around in it a few times to get the lie of the land and tamp down the new mattress when I saw Irene looking at me thoughtfully. I knew exactly what was coming next.

You see, there is one privilege we accord you humans, a little trick we use to calm your fears at being adopted by a new carer, to make you comfortable and help ease you into your new life. We allow you to name us, and sure enough, Irene looked at me and uttered those fateful words, 'Now, what shall we call you?'

I had strong thoughts on this of course. A name is such

a statement of one's core qualities as a dog. One option I liked was a name that paid tribute to my father's athletic prowess. 'Flash' perhaps, or 'Streak' or even the slightly more esoteric 'Shazam'. 'Comet' was nice too.

Alternatively, I could happily accept a name that reflected my proud Mexican heritage with 'Aztec' or 'Zapata' or even the more diminutive but no less distinguished 'Taco'. Yet more than any of those, my innermost desire was a name that went down a more attribute driven path, one that reflected my keen, philosophic and scholarly mind.

I immediately discarded 'Kant' of course. Although I have nothing against his thoughts on transcendental idealism, I just know that standing in a public space and shouting 'come here Kant' might lead to an awkward moment or two.

But 'Plato', for example, I thought perfect, or 'Sigmund' or 'Bertrand'. In time I could probably even grow to love 'Nietzsche'.

Knowing full well that we have the power to influence our human's thought processes, I looked straight into Irene's eyes, sending her telegraphic suggestions on the names that I believed best suited me. She looked straight back at me and after a few moments of contemplation, no doubt selecting from the options I had sent her, she smiled broadly. I knew my message had got through. I was in for something impressive and intelligent and illuminating. 'I know', she said, 'we'll call you Fred!'

My ears dropped and my tail drooped.

There is nothing wrong with the name Fred, of course.

There are millions of wonderful Freds in this world, two-legged and four-legged. But to me, Fred the dog is a drooler, shoe eater, cat chaser, lawn digger-upper, water bowl upsetter, carpet chewer, knee humper.

All perfectly acceptable canine qualities of course but none that inspired a bloke to higher thought or nobler cause.

I would no more chase a cat than chase my own tail (standard Fred behaviour). To me, a Fred is a lazy, lolloping Labrador, or frantic, frenzied Fox Terrier or a big, belly-bouncing Bassett. But me? A Fred?

I who have noble bloodlines dating back to the Incas

on one side and the Saxons on the other. I who am thoughtful, introspective and wise. I who would rather spend my waking hours pondering the intricacies of life than the inner workings of a Kong.

Really, humans sometimes just have no perspicacity!

But Fred it was, and all I could do was accept the indignity of being taken for a common, working class, low-IQ mutt with no ambition greater in life than trying to lick his own arse. Dejectedly, I walked back to my bed, head hung low under the weight of this newly conferred mediocrity.

Irene watched my performance closely. The lowered tail, the droopy ears. I was giving it one last go, trying to reboot the telepathic connection, to de-bug the drop out and get the lights flashing green again.

'No', she finally said, shaking her head slowly, 'you are not really a Fred are you? That's a bit of a common name and you're not a common little fellow, are you? You are special, different from other dogs. You need a name that lives up to that.' I ran back to her, tail wagging. We were back online.

I sat on the sofa next to her, turning this way and that, preening a bit to give her a look at my stronger side. Perhaps if she got a good look at the poise, the personality, something might inspire her?

She stroked my chin and started to think out loud. 'I remember Grandma telling me that when her father came out here looking for gold, he teamed up with a partner who'd come all the way from Paris, France. Grandma used to say that he was handsome in an unusual way, this French man.

Distinguished looking because he was very different looking. Like you! He had quite a long nose. Like you! He had short, stubby legs and a body that stretched long over them. Like you! What was his name...oh yes, I remember. She said his name was Monsieur Beauregard Bouvier!'

I was not sure where this was heading. All this Euro esoterica sounded a bit pretentious to me. A complicated French name is all very well for your pompous, salon-pampered poodle but how would it suit a homegrown hybrid like me, your typical Aussie All-sorts?

Then, with her next words, the wisdom of her ways

made themselves apparent. 'You see, Beauregard means 'handsome to look at', 'a beautiful outlook'. It also means 'highly respected'. I think that's you!'

Genius! Bloody brilliant! My beloved charge had summed up many of my finest qualities in the one name.

I wagged my tail furiously and licked her hand. Reward based training is the only way with humans.

Beauregard sounded impressive and respect worthy. 'Yes', she smiled, scooping me up and planting a kiss on my forehead. 'That's who you are. You are my Beauregard. My beautiful boy. From now on, you are my Beau!'

CHAPTER 5

Armed now with a name a bloke could throw about with pride, life with Irene was turning out to be just as loving and enjoyable as I had hoped. Gentle strolls morning and evening. Lazy afternoons by her side on the sofa.

Generous servings of boiled chicken and rice, or brawn and biscuits or liver with lashings of love. Plenty of pats and conversation that went late into the evening.

Irene would tell me about her childhood, her days as a young bride, show me pictures of her husband Lesley, now in a care home, and talk continuously of her past. Sadly, Les and she had no children and her two sisters, Beryl and Dorothy were both gone.

Other than Les, her only remaining human family was a nephew. 'Dottie's little boy', she called him, whom she had not seen in several years. She'd reminisce about the past with a sad smile on her face, staring into the fire. I'd listen, coaxing her on with gentle nudges and little licks.

I realised early on that if I looked straight into her eyes as she spoke, if I made it obvious that I was interested and listening intently, she felt as if she had a caring companion by her side and a little of her loneliness would evaporate.

Worth remembering, that. If your dog stares straight into your eyes it's not, as so many of you think, that he's thinking of food (although of course, nothing strengthens a shared experience as effectively as a shared snack or two).

No, staring is our way of telling you that we are here for you, you are not alone, and we will always be by your side. Always!

I truly loved Irene. She was kind to everyone she met, generous with what little she had, and a heart larger than the head of a Great Dane with a pituitary problem. These were happy, contented times when the companionship between us was as warm and sincere as any relationship between a dog and his charge can be.

Of course, she could not fully understand everything I said to her, but humans can be taught about 30 words successfully and I started on her training early.

I taught her 'time to eat', 'time to walk', 'time to visit the lemon tree', 'time to just sit quietly, side by side and bask in the joy of togetherness'. She was a quick learner.

Don't believe all that nonsense that you can't teach an older person new tricks. That they can't learn anything new after the age of 45. Patience and perseverance is all any relationship needs!

Most mornings we would head out to the park where I'd run about with my neighbourhood friends, Cassie the German Shepherd cross, Indy a sort of miniature Doberman thingy and Mika the madcap Maltese.

The park was not far from our home. Down the street, across a wide flood water drain, past a row of local shops, right at the lights and there it was, my playground and Irene's social hub.

She'd sit on the bench, talking to her friends Lizzie (Cassie's mum), Doris (Mika's mum) and Alma (Indy's mum). From the park, Irene and I would visit the local shops. We'd walk side by side, stopping to talk to passersby who wanted to give me a little pat or quiz Irene on my breeding.

'A bit of a Nobby's Mixed Special is he?' some would ask with a snigger. 'Got an Arnott's Assorteds there have you Irene?' 'Bit of a Henry Adams party-pack, that one!'

To these comments and questions, Irene would throw out her chest and haughtily deliver the words I never got tired of hearing. 'He's very special', she'd say. 'He's a Chippet'

How brilliantly she'd summed up the complexities of my parentage in a single word. Then, without any further explanation, off we would go, stepping tall, heads held high.

Irene would visit her local greengrocer, her milk bar, her friends at the newsagents. I'd wait patiently outside while she went in for a weekly supply of Prunes and Vita Brits, Woman's Own and Wonder Soap.

Then, it was off to my favourite establishment, Len the Butcher. I'd watch through the big plate-glass window as he weighed out the sausages or chump chops or chicken breasts or whatever delectation Irene had planned for us that evening. Sometimes, Len would slip me a ham hock or a beef bone and I'd trot back to the house with it in my mouth, proud as a Cocker that's just won big at Crufts!

Afternoons were 'quiet time' as we dozed in front of the TV, lulled to sleep by the somnambulant sounds of her favourite soap operas. Then, a short evening stroll, dinner in the kitchen, and our cosy fireside chats.

At bedtime, after a quick visit to the lemon tree, I'd settle down at her feet, on the duvet in Summer and under it in winter, and off we'd drift into the deep, wrapped in the uninterrupted slumber that comes only with true contentment.

The only variation to this routine came on Sundays, Tuesdays and Fridays when we'd go off to visit her beloved Les at the Cosy Nook Care Home. As best I understood it, Les had gone into hospital for a simple hip replacement but something had gone wrong. He'd suffered a minor stroke that left him semi-invalided.

Irene could not cope with him at home, he being a big heavy bloke and he was not able to do much for himself, so after much soul searching, they had decided that it would be better for all if Les got the professional care he needed 24 hours a day.

For some ridiculous reason, dogs (other than those termed 'working dogs' which is most insulting. Given the constant supervision people require, all of us are working all the time) are not allowed onto public transport. It makes me laugh.

We are not the ones who rip up seats.
We do not spray rude graffiti.
We do not leave chewing gum on the hand rails.
We do not urinate in the corners.
We do not talk loudly on mobile phones.
We don't leave refuse behind or drink or smoke or shout obscenities at other passengers who displease us.

Yet, we're the ones banned from catching the bus or train.

Hypocrisy, thy name is Human.

Given this difficulty, Irene would call for a PetCab and

off we'd go to visit Les. Often, he'd be wheeled out to a sunny bench where Irene and he would sit side by side, arm in arm, just happy in each other's company, not needing to say much.

I took to Les immediately. He smelled of Old Spice and Sloan's Linament and Orange jelly with just a hint of a Bex powder about him. An old school Australian, always open to giving a bloke a fair go, irrespective of breed, colour or length of coat.

'Thank you for looking after my old chook', he'd say to me, nuzzling me under the chin with his good arm. 'She needs you laddie. You keep her happy.'

I'd watch the two of them sitting there, holding hands, smiling at the world, underscoring the point that true understanding needs no words. I may have, up to this point said some unkind (but necessary) things about you humans.

But let me also say this.

When you get it right, you get it very right.

When you put aside judgement and bias and just give

yourselves over to the pleasure of just being who you are, of enjoying what you have and the company of those who mean most to you, there is no more creature in the animal kingdom that's more loving or likeable.

You are capable of so much goodness and understanding. When you let those qualities rise above the fears and uncertainty that sometimes well up within you, well that's when you are at your best, a real delight to have around.

That's when we are proud to call you 'our best friends'.

When they were together, no matter what life had once thrown at them, Les and Irene radiated that wonderful positivity that comes from knowing your glass is always half full, no matter what.

They had discovered the secret to happiness that we dogs have long known.

Les and Irene. Where there is warmth,
who needs words?

Chapter 6

Life just flew by. I cannot tell you exactly how long this happy period lasted. Time means little to us.

You humans are ruled by your clocks and calendars, diaries and dates. You seem focussed on the passage of time which is sad because, as we see it, that means you are obsessed with the past.

You allow your past to shape so much of who you are today. You wallow in the pleasures and pain of that which has been and gone. Of friends you will never see again, laughter you will never recapture, or sadness you need never relive.

You believe that your memories enrich you when in reality, memories can do little more than leave you with a dull longing for that which can never be experienced again.

Saddest of all, it leaves you with the inevitable heartache, the self chastisement of 'if only I had said this, or done that...!'

Come on, wake up, it's not that hard.
The gone is called gone because it has gone!

We dogs do not fixate on yesterday because we know that one cannot affect the past. All one can affect is the present.

Which is why we live in the here and now. We let the past pass and we never fret about the future. If tomorrow brings the same contentment, well-fedness, the same routine we have today, then we are happy.

This may sound limited to you, overly simplistic and lacking in aspiration. Yet we have arrived at this enlightened state because we have learnt the one absolute truth that time tries to teach us all: the lower your expectations, the higher your chances of contentment. We are held back by neither the agonies of yesterday or the apprehensions of tomorrow.

Try it. Life suddenly becomes much brighter.

So, while I cannot tell you in years or months how long this halcyon period with Irene lasted, I can tell you that it was long enough for me to notice, day by day, that Irene was getting a little older, a little more unstable on her feet, a little more forgetful.

Walks grew shorter, meal times were a bit more erratic, getting out of bed seemed to get a little harder every day.

I could of course remind her when she left the front door open and unlocked, or lead her to the park when she grew unsure of the way, or when she'd left the kettle to boil too long, or let her know when the phone rang, but I worried about how long she could continue to live in our little home safely and independently.

I can also tell you that during this period, I grew from puppyhood to manhood. My body changed. I grew longer, (though not much taller). My chest rounded out Whippet style, and the full blossom of male-dom descended upon me, making themselves evident to all. It is ironic that while I may have inherited my mother's attitudes, I inherited my father's attributes.

Often, I would catch Irene starting at my rear end and

I'd hear her say, 'We need to get something done about those Beau. But I don't trust doctors. My Les went in for something they said was routine and he never came home again. So perhaps, we'll just let you keep growing a bit more.'

This was fine by me, though I have to admit, the Whippet-sized bits between my Chihuahua-sized legs made sitting on my haunches truly uncomfortable. I either sat or lay on my side. Anything else brought tears to the eyes.

On the upside though, Irene never took me to that place where they stick needles in animals or chop your claws off.

Winston, the British Bulldog that lives next door, butch and brave as he is, trembles uncontrollably when he recounts his hospital horror stories to me. How they put a chip in his neck, how they made him swallow unpalatable pills and most unbecoming of all, how they took his temperature.

Can you humans not see how demeaning it is to a proud and noble beast to have someone fossicking around his posterior, probing where no man has probed before?

Disgraceful. Worse, disrespectful!

My fears about Irene grew more profound every day.

Sadly, there is one immutable fact one has to accept when one chooses to take charge of a human. One day, time or infirmity will separate you.

When the day comes, it is our responsibility as their carers to make sure we let them go with as much dignity and comfort as possible. A huge sadness of course, but the alternative is never to let a human into your life and that's no alternative at all.

After all, as we dogs say, the joy of a single beef bone is worth more than a lifetime of stale biscuits.

See? Half full, our glasses. Always!

Winston of the BBC (Bulldog Broadcasting Corp.)
the source of my daily news bulletin

CHAPTER 7

Change is inevitable of course and change came to our little household one day when the first warmth of summer enveloped Ballarat in a bright burst of dazzling sunlight. I walked into the kitchen one morning to find Irene as excited and nervous as a Rottweiler on a road trip. She was standing on a chair, reaching up to the highest shelves. The shelves where she kept her 'best China', as she called it.

'Oh Beau, it's so wonderful. I got a call from my nephew Barry, Dottie's little boy. He's coming for tea today. I have not seen or heard from him in five years and out of the blue, he called to say he wanted to come see his old Aunty Irene.'

'Now where did I put those cake tins?' With that, she busied herself mixing up the batter for her famous Passionfruit Jellyroll (Highly Commended at the

Ballarat Daughters of Gold Miners Cake show she'd once told me) and laying out her best tea cups.

I absorbed this information with mixed feelings. I was happy to think that Irene would at last have the human company she craved, someone who would do the things for her that I could not; ring for the doctor, get her tablets from the chemist, get her hot water bottle when she needed it.

Unfortunately, while we dogs are blessed with an abundance of heart and soul, our appendages are not best suited to fetching and carrying and doing up buttons for arthritic fingers. Having someone she could trust, someone who could supplement my emotional caring with a bit of physical looking after, would be a real blessing.

But why had Barry not called before? Where had he been all this time? And why now?

Irene herself gave me the answers to the questions. Unlocking the only cupboard in her living room that could be locked and pulling out the biggest, silver teapot you could ever imagine, she twittered on.

'This is pure sterling silver Beau', she explained while polishing it furiously. ' It belonged to my Grandmother and I think today is a special enough occasion to bring it out. After all, Barry says he's driving all the way from Ararat! I never realised that he's been living there. Wonder what he's been doing all this time?'

The penny dropped. 'Five to Ten' most probably, I wanted to shout out to her. You see, dear Irene had made it sound as if Barry was driving in from a Galaxy Far, Far Away, a bijou settlement inhabited exclusively by the wonderful, worldly and wise, but I knew a thing or two about Ararat.

My mate Moby the bipolar, bicycle-chasing bi-breed had spent his early years in Ararat and often talked about it. A fine upstanding little town of course, full of decent hard-working people, but hardly known for the breadth of its cultural diversity or the magnitude of its employment opportunities. What would Barry have been doing there for so many years? Why had he never made contact before? Why now was he suddenly free to come and see his Aunt?

Remembering Moby's rundown on the town's most outstanding features, it all fell into place. Clearly Barry had, until recently, been a full-service guest at Her Majesty's most excellent Bed and Breakfast, the Ararat Prison!

This did not feel good to me. I started to imagine the worst. Barry could be a scoundrel, a blackguard, a crook? Could I trust him to run around the house unattended and not rip up carpets? Of course, I stopped immediately to give myself a good talking to.

People prejudge people, I reminded myself.

We dogs do not.

We never give a person a bad name and hang him.

We take all creatures as we find them, free of partiality or prejudice.

We judge for ourselves, unencumbered by the misdirections of gossip or rumour.

Presumption is a dangerous human habit which leads you to forming biases before you form well-reasoned opinions and bias is little more than the black art of judging others by what you think they lack. We prefer to take them for who they are. So, wiping my fears from my mind, I waited expectantly with Irene for Barry to make his appearance, ready to accept the man as I found him.

The appointed hour of 3pm came and went. Irene put on another pot of fresh tea.

4pm came and went. Irene reset the table, re-polished the teaspoons.

5pm came and went. Her passionfruit delight was now more Jelly goop than Jelly roll.

Finally at 7pm, the door bell rang. Irene opened it and Barry entered. He was not alone. He'd brought with him a small, grimy backpack and the unmistakable stench of an afternoon spent on a barstool somewhere. He greeted his Aunt with all the affection of a Bull Terrier towards a Burmese short hair. 'So, howyabeenthen?'

Irene gave the man a big hug and rambled on about how long it had been and how much he had changed.

I looked him over carefully. Tall, large and ugly as a Boxer that's fallen face first from a first floor balcony.

His arms were like ham hocks and on them, the brutal, ill-composed scrawls of prison tattoos. His face was lined with the scars of a hundred battles fought. Nose pushed to one side, a brow thick with the blows it had taken.

His clothes looked too small for his body, stretched tight around him, as if he had stepped out of them some time ago a leaner man and found, five years later, that State-sponsored slop was as fattening as it was filling.

Seeing him for myself, I could now size him up accurately.

A con if ever I'd seen one! The man was as uncouth (and as unshaven) as a wire-haired Wolfhound.

Irene though was acting as if he was the cuddliest Yorkie in all Western Victoria. Giggling and chirping with delight, she led him past me to the table she'd laid out so proudly. As he walked by, I took a deep breath of the aura wafting off him. I shuddered.

Stale beer and sweat. Burnt cork, dirty ashtrays, rotten eggs and most damning of all, cat dander.

My nose confirmed my worst fears.

This man was more than just bad. He was cruel!

Trouble had come to visit.

CHAPTER 8

★ ★

I sat in my basket watching Irene pour tea from her silver teapot, so heavy she trembled as she tried to lift it.

'Got nutthing stronger?' Barry stopped her rudely. Irene looked confused. 'I could put another teabag in, if you like?'

Barry's face turned from disinterest to scorn. 'No beers in the back there', he asked pointing to the kitchen, 'no leftover Christmas Sherry?'

Irene looked crestfallen. 'Oh, I'm so sorry. There's no alcohol in the house Barry. We may have some Sarsaparilla somewhere.....'

Barry shook off her attempts at making amends.

'S'arright' he growled, 'just pour us a cuppa.'

I don't know why I had expected more. When one has been a long term guest of the Government, one's social graces are bound to suffer.

For a moment or two they sat there, not knowing what to say next. She sipped. He slurped. Then, looking around, he spoke. 'Live here alone, d'ya?'

'Well since your uncle Les went into care, it's just me and Beau here,' she replied. For the first time, he turned to look at me.

Let's be honest now. For every human who likes dogs, there are as many who dislike us. It's hard to explain. Perhaps they fear being shown up by us or feel they cannot prove themselves worthy of our company?

Perhaps they feel diminished by our devotion, incapable of reciprocating? Who knows?

We dogs can spot a dog-disliker a mile away. They cross the road when they see us coming, or pull their children away from us or, most demeaning of all, pinch their noses as we walk by. Barry was very obviously not a member of the 'Cuddle your Canine' club. He studied me closely before opening his mouth. 'Funny lookin' mutt. Looks like a tube of toothpaste. One a' them little travel size ones that's been squeezed in the middle.'

I was truly appalled. Were there no limits to the depravity? Instinctively a little growl of displeasure rumbled in my throat. To underscore the inaccuracy of his comments, perhaps it's time I gave you a honest description of my bearing and stature.

I have my father's long body shape and measure 91 cms or 36 inches from tip of nose to start of my tail. That's about the length of a Stretch-Dachshund.

My tail is another 24 cm, or 9 inches giving me the overall length of a slightly over-extruded Corgi or an underdeveloped Basset.

Most distinctively, I am 30 cm or 11 inches from just nose to nape of neck alone. I have often heard my neck being described as swan-like. I presume that's another way of saying it is slender and graceful.

I have a long pointy face, a sharp snout and long, narrow ears. I have my father's deep barrel-like chest, 52 cm in circumference and a slim 40 cm waist. (Presumably the reason for his 'squeezed in the middle' comment).

But there my conformity with Whippet ends and my uniqueness begins.

Because, underpinning this long, somewhat bullet-shaped body, I have my mother's legs, just 15 cm from shoulder to paw pads. To sum up, I am about 3 feet long, 9 inches tall and round all over.

You see now why I take umbrage at being called a travel-size tube of toothpaste?

True, I am low slung, with minimal ground clearance. But then, all high performance bodies are! Think Formula 1, rather than High-Rider. We are engineered to hug the road rather than just bounce around above it.

My low centre of gravity gives me immense manoeuvrability and a turning circle a Border Collie would die for. Like any well-designed projectile, I am shaped to minimise wind resistance. My ears sweep back when I am at full throttle and stand tall when I need to create drag.

My nose and neck jut out long and slender, with the air piercing properties of the Concorde. My coat is smooth and my tail is as thin and firm as the business end of a bull whip.

Not surprisingly, I have heard people liken me to instruments of great speed and power such as 'pocket rocket', 'torque-y torpedo' and 'mini-missile'.

But a travel size tube of toothpaste? Clearly the man is as blind as he is boorish.

To complete the picture, my face, head, throat, shoulders, legs and haunches are a beautiful tan and black brindle.

'Tiger skin' the uninitiated call it. Dare I say that these are markings as remarkable as they are rare. My neck and back, sides and tail are a jet black, as if nature had slung a long saddlecloth, satin smooth and shiny, over me. Imagine if you will an inverted glass of Guiness. Dark on top. A rich tan below.

I stand, eight and half kg of well-rounded muscle, with proud chest, chiselled features and large brown eyes that Irene says look as if I can see right into her soul.

Please understand, there is no ego here. I am not trying to portray myself in an overly flattering light. But Irene did once remark that had Stubbs or Landseer been alive today, they'd be calling round in no time.

Finally, I am thin-coated and thin-skinned as are all Whippets but underneath that, I come armed with my mother's fiery Latin temperament. We don't take kindly to fools, prodding fingers or pushy Pugs panting in our faces.
Most of all, we abhor insulting behaviour and bad manners.

To be fair though, there was one further test I had to put Barry through before I consigned him to the disreputable scrapheap known as 'dog hater'. I walked up to him with a little low growl, nothing aggressive you understand, just enough to let him know that I would have none of this rudeness in my house when, much as I had expected, once he saw Irene was not looking, his leg shot out swiftly and suddenly, the reinforced toe on his Doc Martens caught me a nasty blow on my rib cage. I yelped more out of disgust than pain.

I knew now for sure that before me stood the most heinous human of all. Barry was a dog kicker!

CHAPTER 9 ★

★

As Irene started to clear away the tea things, Barry's eyes, sly and shifty, started to wander about the room. He pointed to the silver teapot Irene was carrying away. 'What's that worth then?'

Irene, was still lost in the joy of having rediscovered a long-lost relative. She only saw his presence. I saw the pretence.

'Oh, it's priceless this. Pure silver. Belonged to my great-grandmother. Great-grandfather came out here prospecting. She carried it all the way from the old country and she treasured this above all else.'

'Yeah, yeah', Barry yawned, 'but what's it worth? Ever had it valued?'

'No need,' smiled my innocent, 'it will never be sold. One day, it will...well, I suppose..it will come to you.'

My heart sank. She was as good as waving lamb shanks at a Labrador. I could see the drool forming.

'Yeah, and this house too?' he asked, barely able to control his greed.

'Well, I have no one else,' she shrugged. 'It's just Beau and me, so one day, yes I suppose, the house too. But as long as I have him, this place suits us fine. We're not going anywhere in a hurry are we boy?' she smiled at me.

Barry turned to look at me again, this time with a smirk as insincere as the smile on a Siamese. 'Ahh,' he intoned, 'who couldn't love a little chap like our Beau?'

Our Beau? This was going from bad to worse. Clearly the swine had evil designs on my poor Irene's meagre possessions.

The full extent of his intentions were made clear when he next spoke. Feigning concern with all the deceit of a duplicitous Dingo, he took Irene's hand in his.

'Ya all alone here? S'it safe? Ya feel ok? I reckon you need someone to look after ya, Aunty Irene. To be here for ya. Take ya to see my dear uncle Len.'

'Les', she corrected him.

'Yeah, that's what I said. Les. Hearing not too good eh?'

The devious illegitimate individual!

'Ya know, I could stay here a few days, if you wanted... keep you company an that.' Irene turned to him, all concern.

'Have you nowhere to stay? Your own house?'

'Nah, I've just been..eh..sort of poking about here an' there. Travelling, ya' know. Like..eh...mustering..an..an..shearing'. (Innocent people I'd no doubt!) Reckoned tho' it was time to come back to good ol' Ballarat. Got plenty of mates who'd be chuffed to put me up of course. But they're not blood, are they? Not me own family...like you are.'

How I wished at that moment that I had taught my darling the words for 'don't believe a word of this nonsense and chuck the conniving swine out!'

Honestly! The man was more full of shit than a constipated Corgi. For a moment, Irene hesitated. 'Well, it's not a big house. Just my bedroom and the sofa bed in the spare room.'

'All I've got is this one bag,' he countered. 'Don't need much space.'

'I don't know', Irene demurred. But my joy was short lived. Her generosity would be her undoing.

'Well, you are my only family and it would be nice to have someone to talk to...so yes, of course, you stay here until you get yourself set up, proper like.'

My darling innocent one! She reminds me everyday that of all your human qualities, the two we animals love most are innocence and grace.

Innocence is your ability to see the good in others. Grace is how you cope with being proven wrong. Innocence, is you feeding the grizzled old alley cat that comes round yowling for food. Grace is how you forgive him for eating your budgerigar.

Innocence makes you generous, caring, and accomm-odating; all essential ingredients for successful human/animal co-existence. Grace is the tolerance you extend to those of us non-humans who dig up your lawn or eat your crops or shit on your windscreens.

What we dogs find amusing is how, quite often, you find it easier to extend those qualities to us than to others of your own kind. Still, that's a human thing and I leave that to you to sort out. I had enough worrying to do about our new house guest.

'You take my bedroom, it's a little bigger and I'll use the spare room. Don't suppose it'll be too long before you find your own place,' Irene smiled generously.

'Great', he replied, kicking off his shoes and stretching back on the sofa. He put his legs up across it and spread his arms out wide. Clearly my days of stretching out on it were over.

'So', he glanced up at his Aunt, 'whatsfer dinner?' he asked gracelessly.

CHAPTER 10

We dogs have a saying. 'It takes just one ear mite to turn ecstasy into eczema'. How true that turned out to be at Chez Beau and Irene. Within days, Barry had turned our happy little home into his personal garbage bin.

Irene's bedroom, now Barry's domain, soon resembled a pig sty. Filthy clothes strewn around the place, empty cigarette packets and old newspapers on the floor and when there was no more room there, he expanded.

His vile smelling ashtrays, overflowing with cigarette butts made their way into the living room where they met up with his stash of empty beer cans to form what I can only describe as a malodorous homage to man's least likeable habits.

Dirty footprints off his muddy Doc Martens soiled the floorboards Irene strove so hard to keep clean. Soiled tissues, greasy paper napkins and smelly socks sprang up around the house like potato vines taking hold of a pasture.

Poor Irene tried her best. She washed, cleaned, dusted, polished and tidied with the single-minded focus of a Kelpie rounding up a recalcitrant ram, but his mess was greater than her dwindling energy.

He'd started to invite his dubious mates over to drink beer and watch the footy, collaring the TV and the lounge, late into the night, irrespective of his aunt's wishes or desires.

They'd curse and howl and carry on, getting louder with each emptying six pack. Worst of all, most nights, before the booze took him off to sleep, he'd walk out into my back yard and relieve himself on my lemon tree! Irene was flustered, unhappy, greatly disturbed but knew not how to deal with it all.

Then, the real troubles started. 'Have you seen my grandmother's silver teapot Barry?' she asked him one morning. 'I can't think of where I've put it'.

'Goin' a bit soft are ya?' he dared to say to her. 'Forgettin' stuff now?'

'Can't find my mother's opal bracelet anywhere Barry. You wouldn't have seen it around would you?'

'Nah...you probably dropped it somewhere. You're going a bit daft, ain't ya?

'Will we go see Les today Barry?' 'Nah, we just went, remember? Really, you'd lose your head if it wasn't stuck to yer neck.'

And so it went on. He dented her confidence, undermined her independence at every turn. Soon, the poor dear started questioning herself.

'I must be getting old Beau,' she said to me one day as we walked to the park. 'Things are just..well..slipping past me. I just can't seem to manage anymore.'

Now, I know exactly what you are thinking. Why didn't I just get my teeth into the thieving swine's backside and send him packing? Why did I not bark and bay whenever he walked into the room, signalling my displeasure and generally carrying on like one of those yappy little Pekinese pork chops?

Well my friends, although I had not quite figured out why, it was clear to me that belligerence was exactly what Barry wanted from me. He used every opportunity to goad me, bait me, get a scratch or a nip out of me. He'd 'accidentally' tip over my food bowl while I was eating. He'd 'accidentally' step on my tail. He'd turn me out into the yard when it was raining and 'accidentally' forget to let me back in.

On occasions when Irene went out leaving me at home with him, his nastiness turned into real cruelty. He'd never hesitate to take a swipe at me, grab me by the scruff and shake me about, chase me with a long-handled broom.

The reasons for his actions revealed themselves one day as I hid under the bed to avoid the ramifications of his foul temper. 'Come on dog', he shouted, 'come out an' take a bite of me, one little nip. It's all I need to get the old bag to get rid of you once and for all. Once I can show her what a dangerous, bloodthirsty little mutt you are, she won't have a leg to stand on and I'll have the vet put an end to yer' faster than you can say Jack Russell.'

Obviously Barry wanted me gone. Somehow, I was an obstacle to something Barry wanted for himself.

Forgive me, but I have to digress here for a moment. As much as we know (and love) about you humans, there are aspects of your persona we find impossible to understand.

Intolerance and vengefulness are at the top of the list.

Yes, we dogs have fights and disagreements, but they are quickly settled. A bit of a telling off, a little nip or two, a bit of fur in the air followed by a tail between-the-legs retreat and all is forgiven and forgotten.

We don't bear grudges, let animosity linger or hate simply for the sake of hating. We fight when something feels wrong. You fight, on the other hand, because it feels right.

I have thought some on this matter and can only surmise that these nasty traits are fed by your insecurity towards that which you think threatens your status quo. You seem wary of anything that challenges you to rethink, perhaps even widen, the boundaries you have defined for yourselves.

Fear means that you evaluate others by the level of discomfort they raise in you, by the distance of the differences between you.

That is why so many humans are uncomfortable with those they think are smarter or resent those they think are richer or make fun of those who speak in a different way. You are far more comfortable in the presence of those who conform closely to your own way of thinking, to your way of living.

In other words, you best practise tolerance when you have nothing to be intolerant about.

Worst of all, and this is what causes the most harm I think, you often choose to believe that different standards in others equates to lower standards in others.

The vegetarian thinks himself holier than the meat eater.

The believer more righteous than the atheist.

The scientist more entitled than the street artist.

The employed more deserving than the unemployed, (whatever the reason for that unhappy state).

To us, seeing oneself as being better, or more deserving than another dog is the start of a disease worse than worms in a Weimaraner. It's the start of bigotry.

You hate that which challenges your own self-assumed state of superiority, the sense of entitlement you have awarded yourself.

Perhaps you feel I am getting a little above myself, a dog spouting on about human failings.

So let me talk dog.

In life there are all sorts.

Proud, protective German Shepherds.
Dutiful, devoted Dobermans.
Empty-headed Beagles.
Intelligent Rottweilers.
Belligerent Bull Terriers.
Peace loving Greyhounds.
Keen, canny Cattle dogs.
Lazy, lugubrious Labradors.

There are those who give service and those who require servicing.

Those that chase for a living, those who chase as a hobby.

Those who guide. Those who need guidance.

Those that are black and curly coated, golden and long-haired, even those who are brown and hairless.

Here's the thing though.

There is no breedism in our world. Don't know the meaning of the word! Differences mean nothing to us!

Shepherds don't gang up on Sealyhams.

Bull Mastiffs don't badmouth Beagles.

Collies don't condemn Cairn terriers.

Inter-breed 'ganging up' seems to be a uniquely human occurrence.

To us, it is the disparities in our backgrounds and bloodlines that make our park as rich and rewarding a place as it is. We could not imagine a world populated solely by snobby Salukis, or arrogant Afghans or bubble-headed Borzois, or worst of all, pretentious little Pomeranians. How dull and uninspiring would that be? Yet you, it seems, would prefer a world where everyone else was more like you? Almost as if you believed the existence of diversity will somehow dilute your DNA, erode your ethnicity.

Wake up people! Difference is how nature makes sure we can survive our own insufferable, individual shortcomings. By adding the flaws of others to our own foibles she creates a stronger, more all-encompassing whole. Diversity makes you, the single entity, a part of something bigger, better, more complete and more meaningful.

Ok, dogma done. Back to the dickhead in the Doc Martens.

Pow wow in the park. From left: Kransky, Fluff, Moby the Maniac, Indy, Tux, Little Tessa, Cassie and Jack. All different. All the same.

CHAPTER 11

As I mentioned earlier, I found Barry's determination to get rid of me a bit perplexing. What was it about me he found so threatening?

I got the full picture one day when Irene was out at a Probus meeting and Barry brought home a friend of his called Slick.

No friend Barry brought home was more appropriately named or looked more disreputable and untrustworthy. Long, greasy hair, beady little eyes, a shifty smile that could easily lull you into letting your guard down. He came dressed in a burgundy shirt and lime green tie. His collar was as grimy as a Mudi in a mud puddle and his tie bore the traces of all the grease that had eluded his thin, evil mouth.

As they talked, it became apparent that Slick was even

more self-serving than Barry himself. They walked around the house, Slick poking his nose into all its nooks and crannies. Finally, he turned to Barry. 'Yeah, it'd be worth a bit. Reckon you can get the old girl out?'

The hairs on my neck stood on end when I heard this.

Barry shrugged. 'Only one thing keeping her here. That little turd dog of hers. Once I get rid of him, what's she need a house and yard for? She'll be that lonely, she'll beg me to move her into one of them places they put old people no-one needs no more.'

So! As simple as that. Beau goes, Irene buckles, Barry makes a bucketload. Ever notice how the more some humans desire, the more devious they become? They both turned to look at me.

I pretended to be enormously interested in the webbing between my toes, as if I had no interest in their conversation.

Remember one thing always. There is no finer actor in this world than a dog that doesn't want to be caught with a piece of your carpet in his mouth. We do stupidity with consummate skill.

'Well?' asked Barry who clearly could barely contain himself, 'whaddya' reckon?' Slick nodded sagely, nosily drawing breath in through the gaps in his teeth. 'About 500k I reckon. Maybe 575k on a good day.'

Barry looked like a Bichon Frise that'd just nicked the biggest baguette in the boulangerie. 'Gee, 500 thousand bucks', he gloated. 'I could do summat' with that. You sure about that?'

'Maaate,' responded Slick turning on his 100 watt salesman smile, 'I've turned over more properties than a cardinal has a choir boy. Trust me. Put this house into my hands and you're as good as made.' My hackles rose. This was worse than even I had expected.

'Yeah, well...I'm gonna' havta' to talk to the old girl. The house is still hers, see.'

"Ahh,' said Slick, 'be smart with that mate. Get her to first open a joint account with you. Easy enough. Tell her that one day, when she can't sign cheques no more, she'll need you, her only remaining relo, to do all that paperwork for her. You'll look after her affairs, make sure the money is well invested. Once your name goes on the account, mate, you're home and hosed.'

'In fact,' Slick continued, rubbing his hands with glee, 'I've got a lawyer mate, who'd be happy to draw up the papers and get it all fixed up. Then we sell this dump, deposit the money into the joint account and you're a made man Barry.'

Barry's eyes glazed over as he gazed into a future cushioned with 500 thousand dollars worth of possibilities.

Slick drew up closer and started his seditious sell. 'Think of it mate', he whispered, 'all those Balinese babes. All those birds and bars in Bangkok. Just waiting for a man like you..they are! Those Brazilian beauties, living it up in the clubs on the Copacabana, those French hotties, topless on the sands of Saint Tropez. They'll be hanging off you like the balls on a Mallee bull, hungry for a little action, hungry for you. That's the good life Bazza me ol' mate! It's what you need. No! It's what you deserve!'

Honestly! The man could have sold hair extensions to a West Highland White! Words poured out of him like honey from a hive, thick and sweet. He was oily and cajoling and Barry the blockhead swallowed it all in one mouthful like a Blood Hound with a bratwurst. Lost in dreams of his soon to be explored sexual prowess, Barry could barely keep the excitement out of his voice. 'So what's that all gonna cost me...eh..I mean my poor Aunt Irene?'

'You know what estate agents charge around here?' Slick asked innocently. 'Nah', the chump replied. 'You tell me.'

'Well, let's see now,' said Slick, eyes a-glint with greed. 'You're a mate and that means everything to me. I'd look after you see? You can always trust me. So, let's say, finding a buyer, organising the advertising and auction, arranging the sale, getting the lawyer to do the conveyancing and paperwork, getting the bankers to open a joint account, doing the leg work, well, I'd say about 35% of the sale price should see me right.'
'How much is that?' asked Barry, more at home with misappropriation than mathematics.

Slick turned on his sweetest smile, lowering his voice to its gentlest whisper. 'Still plenty for you to have the time of your life mate. See, the secret is, you turn your dollars into Rupiahs and you'll be the king of Kuta for the rest of your days. A Bintang's a buck a bottle out there. And I know a bloke who'll get you a great exchange rate, leave that to me.'

Do I need to say more? The basest kind of man! One who would steal brandy from a St Bernard!

They skulked off together, making their hideous plans to steal my darling Irene's house and money from right under her nose. What worried me most of course was knowing that my gentle girl was too nice, too generous, too trusting to say no. Although she'd started to get uncomfortable around Barry she was always going to give him the benefit of the doubt.

Quite often, sitting on our park bench, my head on her lap, she voiced her private fears about her nephew to me. 'He is a bit messy, but I'm sure that'll change', she'd say to me. Or, 'He has taken over the house a bit, but I'm sure he'll find his own place soon.' Or, 'He doesn't work but he always has money for that beer and those awful cigarettes. Wonder where he gets it from?'

Despite these uncertainties, I knew she could no more stand up to a bully like Barry than a Maltese to a Mastiff. If only somehow she could see him for the cur he truly was. If there was some way I could draw back the curtains for her.

That evening I took to my bed, head between my paws

and drove all frivolous matters from my mind. I had some serious, even existential you could say, thinking to do.

Don't be fooled. True visionaries see farther when their eyes are shut

CHAPTER 12

Slowly, despicably, Barry and Slick's evil plans began to take shape. When Irene was out of the house, Slick brought strangers in to appraise and evaluate. His lawyer, as mean-looking and malodorous as mange on a Mountain Dog, came by to get Slick's signatures on papers that needed signing. Surveyors checked out the house and prospective buyers started marching through the place.

Like the cowards they were, Barry and Slick colluded in corners and whispered silently in shadows. 'Don't say anything to the old bat about selling the place', Slick advised Barry. 'Just get her to agree to the joint account first. Once we have that, we have her!'

And all the while I watched and waited and planned.

Finally, the day came when all they needed was for Irene to agree to a joint account with Barry, thereby opening the door to him turning our comfortable little cottage into cold, concealable cash.

Well-coached by Slick and the lawyer, Barry started his pitch one evening during a meal he'd offered to cook for her. I thought Irene might have grown suspicious at this first ever offer of assistance or domesticity, but she was just happy to have someone else do some of the work for once.

I use the term dinner loosely. Really, it was food only fit for a Staffie with no standards. He forked a blackened sausage on to her plate followed by mashed potato that looked to have the consistency of cement. Irene accepted it all with her customary good grace.

Barry started on her almost immediately. 'How long you reckon you can go on livin' here alone, lookin' after yerself like?'

Irene shrugged. 'I don't have an option really, just got to keep going I suppose.'

'Listen', he drew closer, 'one day, you won't be able to

walk to the shops, or pay your bills or sign your bank stuff, will ya? Your arthritis is already pretty bad, ain't it? The pains in your knees and hands?' She nodded. No sense denying the inevitable.

'I could take care of you', he continued. 'Make sure your bills was paid, there was food in the house, look after old Len.'

'Les,' she corrected.

'Yeah, s'what I said, old Les's costs were all paid. You'd never have to worry again. I'd be like...like...yer son or something, ...like ya never had before.'

Oh the chicanery. The cruelty of it. To hit her where it hurt most. Her heart! On and on he went, promising to be there, to care, to protect.

Finally, he ended with the most egregious promise of all.

'I tell ya Aunty, we open a joint account and you won't have to lift a finger ever again. Well, ya probably won't be able to pretty soon. No...you can just sit back, worry free, visiting Len..eh..Les... an playin' with your puppy here. Ya'd like that, right?'

'Well', said my beloved, 'it does sound sensible given I'm not getting any younger and I could use a hand. If you really think it's for the best, let's give it a go. After all, you are my only relative. If I can't trust you, who can I trust?'

Really, has there ever been anyone more pure-hearted put on this earth?

'No worries', Barry concluded. 'I'll get this lawyer bloke I know to set it all up. He'll get someone from your bank to bring all the papers round. You just sign once and Bob's your uncle. No more muckin' about with signatures and bankbooks and balances an' the like.

How about next Monday eh? This banker bloke just needs to hear you say that you are happy to..eh..let me sign for you..ya know..when you can't. That way, it's all set up nice and legal like.'

So! A time frame had been set and the charade was about to begin. I had less time than I had bargained for, but what the heck? When someone declares war on you, you don't demure simply cause its wash day. You just choose your weapon and get ready to face the charge when it comes.

My weapon, I had decided, was going to be the plain, honest truth. The truth about who and what Barry really was.

His true intentions. The true reason he was cosying up to her. I had to unmask him, in front of her very eyes.

I had devised several scenarios which all led me to the same conclusion. Somehow, I had to get Barry to shake Irene to her very core, shock her so greatly, it would clear away the false image she had of the man and stun her into seeing his true character.

Knowing her as I did, there was only one thing I could think of that would stir her sufficiently. There was no other option.

I had to put myself on the line.

CHAPTER 13

The Monday of the proposed meeting with lawyer and banker dawned bright and warm, an innocent everyday-ness about it that belied the life-changing plans Barry and Slick had drawn up for Irene and me.

At 10am sharp, Irene presented herself to us in the living room. She'd taken extra care over her dress and simple makeup. A single strand of pearls floated around her neck. People, important people, lawyers and bankers and the such were coming to her house and old-fashioned pride demanded one put one's best foot forward and one's best silver teaspoons on the table.

The big surprise to me was the efforts Barry had made, presumably to present himself as a reliable caretaker of his Aunt's accounts, solid and sober. He'd dragged a blade over his visage, but carelessly and haphazardly, only managing to look as if he'd somehow distributed the stubble on his chin over a wider portion of his pasty, pudgy face.

He had on a green shirt Irene had washed and pressed for him and one of Les's old ties. There the restraint ended. In preparation for his new life as Playboy of the Western World and no doubt financed by the things he'd stolen from Irene, he'd gone out and bought brand new trousers and shoes.

Sadly for Barry, the absence of any ethical standards was exceeded only by the complete absence of taste. His new trousers were orange in colour with a sharp crease running down the front of them. They were thin and stretchy, a sort of lycra meets Elastoplast and clung to his legs as tightly as the plastic shrinkwrap around a new chew bone. Completely wrong of course. They were a fabric and fashion designed for someone 20 years younger. The fat on his thighs and buttocks bulged through the straining fabric, giving him the appearance of a soon-to-explode mango.

Pleased as he was with his trousers, it hardly matched the pride he felt over the new shoes he had selected to complement this ensemble. Needless to say, they did not!

'The latest thing from Italy these,' he boasted to Irene as he pranced about the living room showing them off. 'Cost a pretty penny I can tell ya, hundreds, but you gotta pay for quality, right?'

The shoes were an ultra-modern woven fabric that in millennial parlance would be called 'dank'. They had velcro tabs rather than laces, thick, red soles and bright, neon blue uppers; colours that clashed with his trousers as fiercely as a 'STAY'-minded Scottie taking on an 'EXIT'-driven English Setter.

I can best sum it up by telling you that his lower half looked as misguided and inappropriate as one of these modern long tails on a German Short Haired.

Dressed though he was to the nines, Barry looked uncharacteristically nervous and on edge. No surprise I surmised. Probably the first time he was fronting a banker without a mask on. Having a stranger here, someone as official as a banker and not party to the deceit he and Slick had cooked up was definitely making him jumpy.

At the appointed hour, Slick and the lawyer arrived, their presence as welcome as distemper in a Dandie Dinmont.

They slunk about the living room while Irene made them tea and put out the Iced VoVos.

Then, a little while later, the door opened again to admit a man I had never seen before. I immediately liked the smell of him. Shoe polish, pomade, a whiff of old-fashioned Eau de Cologne. Trustworthy, I immediately thought to myself. No easy pushover.

He introduced himself around as 'Mr Anthony from the bank' and shook hands with the other three men in the room.

He was tall and lean, an elderly gentleman with an angular face. He had bright, twinkling eyes that smiled at you with a slight look of perpetual wonder. Eyes, you could tell, that had learnt to look through sadness, to the sunlight beyond.

Perhaps because of this, his face was set in a permanent smile, small but knowing, the smile of a life well-intentioned and a world well-understood.

As they shook hands, I saw him sum Barry up in an instant; the outlandish trousers, the misspelt tattoos, the shifty eyes, the ill-chosen shoes. Mr Anthony had obviously seen a thing or two in his time and what he saw was obviously as distasteful to him as the sight of a Kelpie kicking about in a kitty litter tray.

Slick tried to hurry things up. 'Lets get this signed and done shall we? You must have plenty of big bank things to get back to.'

Slowly, Mr Anthony took in the three men, from one to the other. Bonehead Barry. Shifty Slick. Shyster solicitor. I was sure he could smell the collective greed and villainy (bird droppings and snail pellets) as clearly as I could.

'No hurry', Mr Anthony smiled sweetly to all around him. 'I want to make sure Mrs Spencer understands exactly what she is being asked to do before I let her sign anything.'

What a Malinois of a man!

With that, he sat Irene down at the table and slowly and painstakingly explained the consequences of her action to her.

A joint account, he told her, that nominated Barry as the principal signatory meant that Barry would have open access to her money anytime, no questions asked. Moreover, as Barry had applied for an account that only required one account holder's signature and not two, he could withdraw any amounts he wanted, move money around or transfer chunks of it to wherever he chose, without ever having to consult her.

Did Irene understand this? Did she approve? Did she think it a sound idea? Would she agree to this of her own volition?

Mr Anthony had sized up the situation. My sweetheart still had not. She just nodded nervously and smiled. Only when he placed the pen in her hand, did she hesitate and look up at Barry uncertainly.

I could not wait any longer. It was time to act!

Barry started on her immediately, trying to smooth away her hesitation. 'Ya know I'm always gonna be here for ya. I'll only do what ya want me to.. what you feel is right, cause I never want to...' Suddenly he stopped.

He looked about in confusion as the gushing warmth of my wrath splattered across his trouser leg and made its slow and meandering way down to his ankles, trickling down his socks and seeping eventually into the folds of his pride and joy, his spanking-new shoes.

Shocked, stunned by the sensation of squishy liquid on his shin, he looked down in amazement and and let out a howl of fury. 'Fuck me!' he screamed to the world, 'the little shit's gone and pissed on me new Pradas!'

I had intentionally aimed high before discharging my duty and was delighted to see a large yellowing stain starting between knee and ankle and dripping, almost artistically, down towards his feet. It permeated the flimsy fabric of his expensive new trousers and turned the bright blue hue of his new shoes into a pleasingly hideous shade of bile green.

From there, it dripped its way through the weave in his uppers, permeated the fancy air vents in his soles, and made its way down to his feet, finally settling around his toes in a pool of pleasingly aromatic, and dare I say it, fitting punishment.

When what had just happened finally got through his thick skull, his howl of fury turned into a fit of reckless rage. 'Fuck me, fuck me, fuck me', he shouted loudly and repeatedly, hopping about on one leg, thereby splashing the elixir of my retribution even further. The others, unaware of the justice I had just meted out, turned to stare at him in surprise, shocked at his outburst.

Irene spoke first. 'Barry, language!' But Barry was beyond reach. All he did was hop about screaming in fury. 'He's peed me Pradas, he's peed me Pradas, the little shit's peed me Pradas!'

I don't know what infuriated him the most. The injustice of his Aunt's admonishment or the indignity of the banker's laughter. The surprising volume of vengeance I had managed to unleash, or Slick unable to contain his sniggering? Whatever it was, I just closed my eyes and waited for the response I knew I'd get.

As we dogs well know, once a kicker...!

Sure enough, drawing back his dripping foot as far as it would go, Barry lashed out forcefully, his now sloshy new shoe catching me on the ribcage with all the ferocity his rage-ridden body could deliver.

I flew through the air, a good 5 or 6 feet, hit the side of the wall near the table where a stunned audience was taking in this unexpected aerial action and finally, slid down the wall, landing by Irene's feet with a loud and weighty thump.

Of course, I made sure I had the sound effects to go with it.

I yelped and howled, whimpered and bayed like a Halden Hound on heat. It did not require much preparation, tell the truth. I really hurt like hell.

The first thing I heard was Irene letting out a scream that could have been heard all the way from Ballarat to Brown Hill. 'Noooooo!!!', she screamed as I lay unmoving on my side, as still as a Pointer that's spotted a partridge.

Then, quivering with rage, she picked me up tenderly and rose to face Barry. 'You kicked my dog! You kicked my little Beau! You kicked a dog! What kind of man are you? How could you ..be so...so cruel, so..so..brutal? How can anyone kick a dog?'

Barry, the thick head that he was, heard nothing. He picked up one of his ashtrays, the heavy bronze one with 'Welcome to Bendigo..the Big Smoke' etched into it and advanced on me with murder in his eyes.

'I'm gonna kill that damn dog....so help me I'm gonna pulverise the little...' Before he could finish, Irene had flung herself between us and stood there glaring at Barry, fire emanating from her nostrils.

As I had anticipated, when the milk of human kindness goes sour, it turns into an acid more caustic and cutting than any other. Irene, freed at last from the restraining hand of kinship, was giving Barry the full weight of her feelings.

The shock she had just received, the brutality she had just seen, had pulled the plug she had kept on her emotions and Barry now got the full wash, straight in the face.

'You're dirty, you're drunk, you're uncouth and uncaring. You kicked my dog! You're a bully and thief! You don't care for me, or Les or anyone but yourself. You're selfish and you smell and you are capable of an action as low, as criminal, as base as kicking a dog. You are no relative of mine!'

It finally dawned on Barry that Topless in Saint Tropez was starting to look more like Locked up in Leavenworth. It only inflamed him further. Anger rising, he pushed a heavy, prodding finger at his Aunt.

'Sit down and sign the damn paper before I thump you one, you silly old bag', he shouted, all reason now having flown his menial mind. 'You just wait till we sell this dump of yours and you won't see me for good. See how you get on with no house and no money.'

In alarm, the lawyer hurriedly tried to cough out a warning.

'Shut it Barry, you daft bugger,' shouted Slick. But too late. The truth was out for all to see.

'Sell my house?', said Irene, blinking her eyes in shock. 'Who said anything about selling my house?'

The banker, good and gentle soul that he was, had heard enough. His voice, calm and composed up to this point now took on the edge of a teller who's just spotted a counterfeit tenner in the cash draw. 'I don't like what I'm hearing here', he announced standing up to look Barry straight in the eye.

He then turned to Irene. 'Mrs Spencer, I think you should rethink this whole deal, or' ...and here he turned back to face Barry ... 'better still we should talk to the police. There's something happening here that smells pretty nasty to me!'

He then reached into his pocket and handed Irene a piece of paper. 'Here is my card with all my details. If the police would like me to make a statement about what I have seen and heard here, you hand that to them. I think you'll find that nowadays, the punishment for animal cruelty is as hefty as the punishment for larceny.'

The lawyer realised immediately that all that remained of this drama was the roll of the credits and not wanting to have his name among them, began hurriedly packing up his papers. Barry turned to Slick for support but I could have told him not to bother. Barry was about to get dropped faster than a turd from a Tibetan Mastiff.

May I ask you one final question here? What is it about loyalty, real, heartfelt loyalty that you humans do not get?

The time that deranged Pit Bull got off the leash and went for my mate Tux, Moby the maniacal mongrel and I were right there beside him, no running away.

We have one strict, inviolable rule. When one is in trouble, the others stand by him even when we know that the unpleasantness aimed at one, is going to wash over us all. One gets in trouble, we all lose a bit of fur.

That's what we call loyalty; commitment to the bond that keeps us true to each other, to share in our fortunes AND misfortunes, for mutual good or bad.

Among you lot, commitment seems to be a more fluid commodity. One based more on what you can get rather than contribute.

You think I'm being too severe? Think of the Christmas Cockapoo that's back at the shelter by Easter? The ex-partner that failed to deliver on expectations? The friend forgotten when his needs became greater than yours? The relationship broken because keeping it together was just 'too damned much like hard work!' Are these not all realities of your life?

In your world, loyalty lubricates a relationship that is already running smooth. Commitment is what you make as long as you are making something out of it. Our allegiances are absolute. Yours seem optional.

As if to prove my point, now that Barry was as useful to him as an ATM without a dispensing slot, Slick started sliding shiftily towards the exit, his dreams of 35% having preceded him out the door. Barry tried to stop him but I could have told him it was no good.

Displaying that well-known human betrayal of deserting a friend in need, Slick was gone in a flash, faster than Fernando Blue rounding the 200m bend at Wentworth Park.

Irene, still heaving with emotion and now realising the full extent of the trap she had almost been led into, calmed herself and looked at the banker.

'There will be no need for the police Mr Anthony, but perhaps you could advise me on a good lawyer who could help me with a new will? You see, Barry will be vacating this premises immediately. He will leave my house in the next 15 minutes and never show his face here again.

A man capable of kicking a poor defenceless dog is not a man I could trust, respect or allow into my home.' Then with the proud spirit of her gold mining forefathers now coursing heatedly through her veins, she turned towards Barry one final time.

'Pack your bags and hit the road buster! And you better make bloody sure I never see your fat arse around these parts again.'

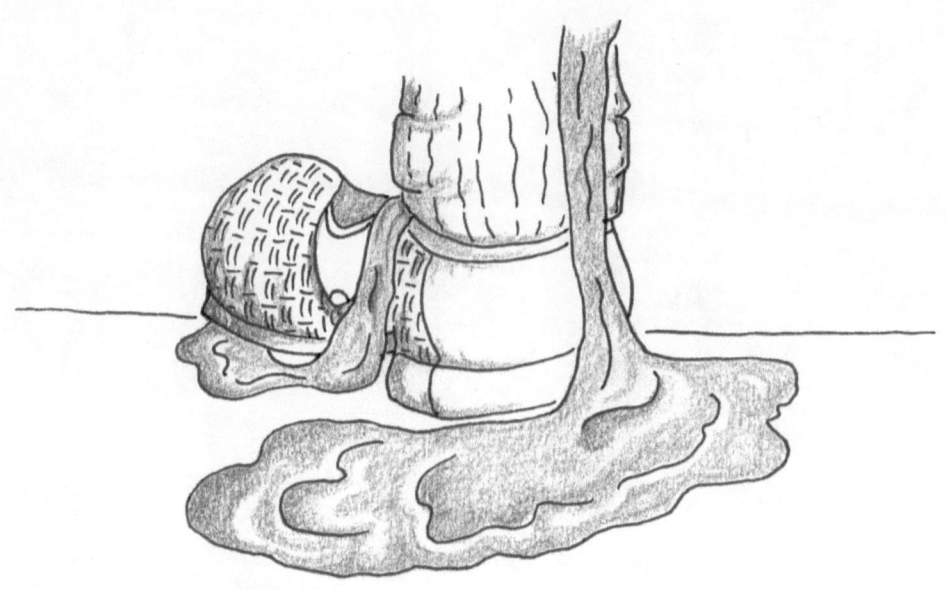

Let justice flow

CHAPTER 14 ★

Bliss!

Peace and Pine O Clean.
Love and Lavender Spray.
Serenity and Sugar Soap.

Let me explain. Within minutes of realising that he was as done and wrapped as a doner kebab, Barry had thrown his meagre possessions into his backpack, given me a final evil stare and walked out of our lives for the very last time.

Mr Anthony the banker stayed back to share a cup of tea with Irene. He patted her hand, told her that she had done the right thing and assured her that if ever she needed help or advice on matters relating to her finances or the house, all she had to do was call him.

I have heard people describe bankers as heartless and unfeeling. I can only suggest they change banks. Mr Anthony had turned out to be as valuable as a Husky in heavy snow. When he had gone, and once she had lain me out on the softest pillow in the house, Irene set about getting rid of the last, lingering vestiges of Barry.

With a fury and energy I had never seen in her before she washed the ashtrays and slung out the empty stubbies Barry had stashed behind the sofa. She bleached the bedding he'd slept on, disinfected the TV remote he'd used and threw away the towel she had given him.

Then, she scrubbed the floors, polished the furniture, scoured the bathroom, Ambi Pur'd the drapes and Glen 20'd every nook and corner of the house until all that was left was the fresh, sweet scent of domestic tranquility.

Our house was ours again, filled once more with good feelings and kindness towards all, compassion and companionship.

That evening, Irene lay me on the sofa next to her as she stroked my head and whispered little endearments. 'I am so sorry Beau, to have brought that man into our house, for what he has done to you. How could I have been so blind?'

I moved my tail a little to show that there's no value in revisiting the past and let's just luxuriate in the here and now, blissful and Barry-free.

Truthfully, I would have liked to do a bit more to show her that 'dog's in his heaven, all's well with the world', but I could not. I could barely move. I had not realised just how powerful the rascal's right foot could be.

I hurt across my side, through my chest and all along my back. Breathing was difficult and painful. I was woozy and found it hard to focus on anything. When I tried to lift my head, the room spun and all I could do was close my eyes and hope this would pass by the morning.

As the evening went on though, I could feel my breathing getting heavier and my body stiffening up. Irene kept looking at me worriedly. She kept stroking my back and neck, watching for any sign of improvement. Finally, when it was dark as night outside, she decided she could wait no longer.

First, she rang and spoke to someone in hushed, nervous

tones. Next she called for a PetCab. When it arrived, she wrapped me carefully in a soft, warm blanket and off we went, she sitting upright on the back seat and me lying on her lap. Occasionally she'd look down at me with tears in her eyes.

With every bump and turn the taxi took, more pain shot through my body. Eventually, I must have passed out because the next thing I can remember is lying on a cool, smooth surface with a bright light shining all around me. I knew instinctively that I was in heaven.

Don't you dare laugh at me! You lot believe in Tooth Fairies and Global Equality and Free Trade Agreements. We believe in long walks, plenty of sunshine and beef! So who's the real pragmatist here?

No, I was about to say, I knew I was in heaven because, as I opened my eyes, through the haze, I saw an angel standing above me. I felt it. I was in the presence of someone special, someone heaven-sent.

I have to tell you, I was fine with that. Not scared at all. We dogs don't waste time pondering the 'is there life after death' thing because firstly, we can't do anything about it and secondly, both options; undisturbed sleep or another run in the park, are pretty much what we love doing anyway.

I reckon you'd only regret things coming to an end if you felt you'd wasted the time you'd been given here and because we don't bother measuring ourselves against the achievements of other dogs, nothing we do ever feels like a waste.

I just hope, if one does get another go-around, that we get to choose our incarnation rather than just have it doled out willy-nilly. I wouldn't mind putting my paw up to come back as one of those big wild cats they make those TV documentaries about.

From what I've seen, they live in places where it never rains, among a pack of friends they can rely on, feel no guilt at sleeping all the day, self-exercise anytime they want to eat and eat without having to look around for a can opener. They have no ambition to achieve much; to build a nest or climb higher up the tree or hoard nuts, yet they're the ones we call Kings of the Jungle. Makes you think, huh?

I do hope though that the After Life isn't just a Lotto, left purely to chance. The way my luck's been going recently, I'd probably come back as a lemon tree! (I will spare you my deliberations on Karma or this story will turn into a saga).

I felt comforted in the presence of The Angel, totally at ease.

She had soft brown hair that shone and shimmered as it fell alongside her bright, young face. She had the cheeks of a Cherub, big beautiful brown eyes and skin that just seemed to glow with goodness. And, the final proof of her angelic status, she was, as with every depiction of angels I've ever seen, clad entirely in white, from neck to knee.

Gently, she leaned over me, stroked my nose and whispered in my ear. 'Don't you worry little one. I'm going to make all the pain go away. I'm going to heal you. My name is Dr Angie and I promise, I'm going to make you as good as new again.' As she nuzzled me, I got my first whiff of Arcadia. Kale and Coco Pops. Mint and Matcha chai Latte. Dior and disinfectant. The distinct aroma of clean, healthy compassion. I liked it!
I can't tell you exactly happened next or what they were doing to me. We dogs have always had a better head for the Humanities than the Sciences, but I overheard her delivering her opinion to a colleague

as they stared at a picture she was holding up to the light.

'Fractured T5 and 6, collapsed lung, internal bruising. Who ever did this to the little fellow should be strung up by the scrotum,' she fumed. I concurred of course!

Angie the Angel then gave me something to ease the pain and put something on my snout that made it easier for me to breathe. Finally, they shaved a bit of my hair off a part of my leg and put in a needle. Then, whatever it was they did, my eyes grew heavy, everything went wavy and soft, the lights dimmed, my heart felt light and the pain faded into the distance. I went limp and the world went away.

Can't tell you how long I'd been asleep, but when I woke, I was in a lovely warm bed, a soft blanket over me and a tube pumping something into me. I still felt bruised and sore, but the pain was less sharp, less piercing.

I lay there, wondering what the meal arrangements were in heaven, when Angie the Angel walked up to me, bowl in hand. It was still hard to sit up and lean over the bowl so the Angel fed me with her own hands, piece by piece, patiently and lovingly.

This happened thrice a day, everyday. She took me out to the backyard to relieve myself, carrying me out gently until I could walk a bit for myself. She gave me things to relieve the pain and things to help me sleep. She did more than heal my body.

With her words, she lifted my spirits. 'You really are a beautiful boy aren't you?'

'You have the gentlest eyes I've ever seen.'
'You really are an old soul, aren't you?
'I wish you were part of my family.'

Kind words, soothing strokes, beefy bites. Really, we dogs do not want for much more.

How, you will ask, could I be so cheerful given the sort of experience I'd just had. What can I say?

Yes, we have our Barrys and our Slicks, proof that nature isn't quite done with this evolution thing yet, but they are mere irritations, inconsequential little fleas clinging onto mankind's extremities, trying to suck what sustenance they can from the rich vein of goodness that flows around us.

Fleas to to be flung off and forgotten, never allowed to darken our judgement about everything that's so right with the world we live in. A world with healing Angels and kindly bankers and tender-hearted people like my Irene. People who also believe in kind words and soothing strokes and beefy bites. That's what we should always be cheerful about.

After a few more sleeps, friendly chats with Milly the clinic cat and more ministering from The Angel, I began to feel a lot better. The pain in my side had diminished greatly and wonder of wonders, I could even sit on my haunches comfortably, with none of that painful, squishy feeling I used to have down there in the past. My embarrassment gone, my equilibrium restored. What a miracle worker was this Angel!

Once I could sit up and eat and pee successfully on my own, Irene came to take me home. The Angel gave her a full rundown. 'His fractured ribs are healing nicely and the bleeding in his chest cavity has stopped. Fortunately his lung was not punctured and there is no diaphragmatic hernia. Also, as we agreed the night you brought him in, he's been neutered and chipped, innoculated and dewormed. Give him a few easy days, gentle walks and these painkillers and he'll be as good as new. I promise!'

With that, Angie the Angel gave me a little kiss on the nose, I licked her hand one final time as full and final payment for kindness rendered. Irene and I went home, healthy and happy and together.

And that my friends is where I think my little story comes to its natural end.

I wanted to share it with you simply because I wanted to help you better understand the animal that adopts you. I have related it from my personal perspective, that of a dog, yet most of the tenets here are held dear by cats, hamsters, parrots, rabbits and other four-footed or feathered creatures you let into your heart.

Disappointed? Too simple you think, even a bit naive?

Of course it is! That's the point!

A huge reason for our state of near constant contentment is that we animals take everything at its simplest, most obvious level. Complexity is a human invention; your search for 'true meaning', the 'underlying reason' behind everything you bump into.

Rather than just giving things a good old chew then burying them in the backyard once and for all, you keep searching and questioning, disbelieving and mistrusting. Sorry, but it has to be said, your single greatest folly, is reaching for a 'rational explanation' for everything.

All you get when you try and reach for the unattainable, is anxiety. Reach into the stratosphere for a star and you'll lose a finger to frostbite. Come back down to earth. It's much warmer.

I suspect some of you may be offended by my outspokenness. 'Sick as a dog', 'Work like a dog', 'Dirty as a dog', 'Fight like a dog', and 'Gone to the dogs' you are happy with. But no one, you will scoff, ever says 'As wise as a dog.'

Well my friends, let me ask. How much attention do you pay to what the animal world tries to tell you? Philosophy is not the province of intellectuals; a science, needing theory and thesis. It is simply the ability to articulate and stand by the things that make you truly who you are. And trust me, that's the only way we know how to live.

So, there we are. I'm not sure I can give you much more insight into the mind of the animal that adopts you and I leave you with this final picture.

Irene and I, side by side on the sofa, at peace with the world, wrapped in the wonderful warmth that comes from true contentment. Lucky to be together for as long as the fates allow, just relishing what we have and never wanting more than that which is in easy reach.

As we dogs say: 'Waste no time ascribing happiness to all the things you have not, when all the while, it lies around you, in all the things you've got!'

I promise you my dears, that's more than just doggerel!

À bientôt.

*Milly the hospital cat drops in. Her daily visits helped heal
the hurt and soothe the soul. Friends can do that.*

117

AFTERWARDS ★

★

Before I go, I have one last little bit of dog-losophy to share with you. Never under estimate the power of a beef bone!

You sit there, gnawing away at its smooth, crunchy, exterior thinking things couldn't get much better when suddenly, there's a crack and to your amazement, all this sweet, squishy marrow floods into your mouth, meaty and malty, a flavour beyond anything you'd ever experienced before.

I am telling you this not because I think you have the teeth (or the good taste) to savour a good beef bone, but because, quite simply, life is a beef bone!

There we were, Irene and I happy as we ever thought we could be when 'Crack', something gave and suddenly you realise that all the happiness you have is just a prelude to even greater pleasure. What gave was Irene's back, bending over to get her Lamingtons out of the oven one day and not being able to stand up.

I had been noticing the changes in her for some time. She was growing more feeble, more forgetful, more fearful, day by day. Small, inconsequential sounds kept her up at night.

It got harder to fold the washing. Her fingers struggled to cope with opening jars or buttering toast or doing the crossword. She kept losing her glasses, forgetting to pay bills, opening the door to strangers without first letting me give them a sniff over.

You will recall that at the very outset of this story, I mentioned the responsibility we took on when we take on a human. It is our duty to make sure they never suffer. I knew the time had come for me to man up and do what had to be done.

My opportunity came the next time we went to visit Les. As Irene and he sat chatting on the bench, Nurse Ruth came out to them with two cups of tea. I had met Nurse Ruth before of course. She took care of Les and would often come over to chat, to make sure Les was

warm enough, or, 'do you need another cardie darling?'
I liked her...Vegemite, tawny port and talcum powder...a
robust, reliable lady.

As Irene stood up and moved forward to take her cup
from Ruth, I snuck my head between her ankles and
made sure she could feel me there. 'Silly boy', she cried,
wobbling dangerously as she tried to avoid stepping on
me. 'He's always getting under my feet', she laughed at
Ruth.

Ruth, thankfully built more like a Newfoundland than
a Norfolk, grabbed Irene before she could do any
damage to herself and sat her down on the bench.
Then, she came and sat next to her. 'And how are you
coping with things my darling?' she asked Irene gently.
'Not so good as I'd like', Irene confessed. 'I'm always
worrying about things and I can't do the ironing no
more and I wish Les was there and it all just gets on
top of me.'

Ruth put a protective arm around Irene's shoulders and
leaned in. 'You know my dear, we have very nice couples
accommodation here. You and Les could have your
own little apartment, your own space, your own TV,
your own little kitchenette. You could cook for yourself

or come down and share a meal with the rest of us if you'd like, it'd be your choice. But you would not have to worry about washing or making the beds or cleaning the windows or any of that heavy stuff.'

I wagged my tail and ran around in a couple of circles to show I approved of where this was going. 'Oh that sounds nice', Irene replied.. 'but...I don't know..'

'Come on old girl,' Les nudged her, 'be great to have you with me full time again. Put our feet up, you know..let someone else make the tea for a change.'

Irene turned to him wide eyed. 'But could we afford it Les? A two person apartment and all the services and meals and that...' He cut her off. 'Course we could! We got no debts. Sell the house, bank the money and we could live on that very, very comfortably! Costs less to run one home than two.'

Ruth stood up to take away the tea things and wheel Les inside. 'No hurry darling,' she said to Irene, 'just think about it. Time to let someone take care of you. Comes to us all love.'

'Be lovely to have you here chook, by my side,' Les waved at her over his shoulder.

'Sell the house?'... Irene whispered almost to herself..

* * * * * * *

That evening, Irene sat in front of the TV, still pondering the events of the day, questions running through her head.

'What would I have to do? How would it work? Would there be enough money?' she kept asking herself. I was busy fossicking about looking for that damn piece of paper. Now, where had she put it?

I sniffed about the living room, the kitchen and then on her bedside table I got it. Definite sniff of banker. I sat at her feet, ostensibly chewing on the edge of the card all nonchalant and innocent like. She spotted it and stooped to pick up the card. 'What are you chewing on ? Oh, Mr Philip Anthony....oh yes..that lovely bank fellow. Now I wonder?'

Sure enough, a day after she'd picked up the courage to call, Mr Anthony came round. He complimented her on her mother's hand-painted teacups, ohh'd and ahh'd over her Lamingtons, drank a second cup of tea and then, he got down to business.

The bank would do everything it could to help, he assured her. He would arrange for all the paperwork and legal documentation. He could recommend a good, trustworthy agent. He'd make sure the finances were all looked after.

'We'll put proceeds from the sale into your account Mrs Spencer and arrange for all your bills, both yours and Les's to be paid directly from that. It will more than cover all your costs, the care home, medications, meals and all other incidentals. What's more, you will always have the spending money you need for the little extras that Les and you may want. From what I can see, if you get the sort of price I think you will, you'll never have to worry about a thing.'

What a champion of commerce the man was!

Well, things moved quickly from there. Irene had opted to have an auction and people started coming round to have a look. No-one that really took my fancy until one afternoon, this fine looking Ridgeback, tall and upstanding, led his people into the house; a young couple with a baby.

Irene showed the couple around while cuddling the baby and talking to it. She was a natural grandmother. I heard the couple enthuse over how 'cosy' and 'cheery' and 'comforting' our little house felt.

Rufus, having looked after the young couple since before they were married, had to be more discerning of course. 'It's their first home,' he informed me, 'so I have to make sure it's safe and secure and that they're not taking on more than they can handle, what with the baby and them both working and what not!'

So I showed him the corner in the living room that got the first morning sunlight and the spot in the kitchen where the last evening rays warmed a fellow's heart. I showed him the spot in front of the fire where you stayed toasty without getting too hot, the damp patch in the spare room that was best avoided, the corner of the carpet that was the tastiest.

I pointed out the locks on the front door and the latches on the back and then, as the clincher, I took him out into the backyard. I showed him the flower bed under which he'd find a couple of much-loved shin bones, the indentation in the lawn that cradled a fellow's body just perfectly, the hole in the fence through which Winston and I had our morning chats and finally, for what they call the 'closer', I led him to my lemon tree.

'Have a go at that', I told him. He did and was most pleased. 'Very nice, very satisfactory', he said giving it all one more look around. 'Don't think they could do much better!'

Sure enough, a week later, they made Irene an offer that met her every expectation and with Mr Anthony's smiling approval, she sold up prior to auction.

'Oh, it's wonderful Beau,' Irene beamed down at me once the papers had been signed. 'In 60 days, Les and I will be together again. Forever! There's just one last thing we have to take care of...'

* * * * * * *

One day, as the packers were collecting the few bits of furniture Irene would be taking with her to decorate their new apartment, Irene rang for a Pet Cab and off we went.

'I spoke to that nice Dr Angie last week,' she told me as we rode together. 'She has a surprise waiting for us.'

The Angel was waiting for us in the foyer. 'Do you think it will be alright?' Irene asked her tentatively. The Angel laughed. 'It's going to be absolutely alright Mrs Spencer. Trust me, I know these people'.

She led us into her little office and there I saw a man and woman waiting for us. The Angel spoke to me. 'Beau, I'd like you to meet my Mum and Dad.'

Her parents! Oh joy! She'd had her parents drive all the way from Melbourne, just to meet me. I was pleased as Punch. How important she must think me! Was I really going to become part of the Angel's family?

I first walked up to the lady who was standing by the door looking a little uncertain. May as well put the nervous one at ease first, I figured. Her name was Lisa. She was tall and elegantly dressed, with a smart blue and white scarf around her neck. Whatever I would have to teach her, I thought to myself, deportment wouldn't have to be a part of it. I took a good whiff. Ohhh... Lindt balls and chamomile tea. Roses and Rosemary. Fresh cut grass and Orange Blossom.

Comforting and classy. A very promising start!

I then walked towards the man who had by this time, sat himself on the floor, so we could talk face to face, at my level. I liked that. He already knew who the boss was going to be. He had a beard and hairy legs. The lenses of his glasses twinkled at me as he watched me walk up to him.

He stretched out a hand of his own accord. 'Aha', I thought, 'someone's already taught him the basics of good manners.'

I accepted the hand and held my nose to it. Malt whisky and Krispy Kremes, after shave, and, what was that?....a touch of... a touch of..Coriander? Interesting, I decided. Solid, dependable and just a bit ...well...exotic! I could work with that.

We spent some time getting to know each other while Irene and The Angel looked on. I licked his fingers, he tickled my neck. I rubbed up against her shins. She stroked my back.

At their request, Milly the hospital cat, an old acquaintance from my in-patient days was brought in as a test of my temperament.

I could have told them not to waste their time. We who are true to the philosophy of Stoicism know that living in peace with all nature is the basis of contentment. She was a cat, I a dog. So what? Room enough for everyone!

Finally, after some time for general chit chat and chin chucking, the man and the woman nodded to each other and he rose to address Irene. 'Mrs Spencer, whenever you are ready to move into your new accommodation, we would consider it a privilege to welcome Beau into our family. He'll never lack for care, or attention, or love, I promise you.'

Irene was overjoyed. She thanked him. He thanked her. Lisa hugged me. I wagged my tail furiously. I could not believe my luck! The Angel was going to become my sister!

Before we left, Irene had one final question. 'Will you be changing his name,' she asked. The man looked me over one last time before he answered. 'Absolutely not!'

'Beauregard sounds perfect to me. Beauregard the Bold. Beauregard the Boulevardier. It suits him perfectly. Such a noble fellow.'

To us he will always be Beauregard of Ballarat!'

* * * * * * *

Once Irene had moved into her apartment with Les and was settled and happy, The Angel took me to see her one last time. We kissed and cuddled endlessly. It was quite probably the happiest day of both our lives.

Irene delighted to be with her beloved husband, comfortable and worry free. And me...well... as I looked back and saw them sitting side by side, arm in arm, her head on his shoulder and his cheek on her head, my heart just swelled with pride and joy. She would never again suffer the infirmity or indignity of isolation. I had sent her, with grace and dignity, to a happier, better place.

I turned away, heart full of pride, knowing I had fulfilled my ultimate responsibility as a Person Owner.

* * * * * * *

That same evening, my new charges drove me to their home in Melbourne. I was excited to get on with it, to explore the rest of my life.

The first surprise that waited for me there was the fact that I was going to have a canine sister. I saw her waiting for me behind the grille of the front door as we walked up the drive.

She looked a Kelpie/Border Collie cross. Black all over but with a white blaze on her chest and white socks on her front paws. For a moment I was worried. They're very smart these farm dogs, quite protective of their own and inclined to start rounding up a bloke just when he wanted to settle down to a nice, restful kip.

I need not have worried. Bella was the Kelpie the farmer couldn't wait to give away. About as simple as a one column Sudoku, she was warm and embracing with not a mean bone in her body. She welcomed me effusively, slobber and slippers flying everywhere. A typical Aussie farm girl, as big-hearted as she was broad-beamed.

The house and garden were huge compared to the accommodation I had been used to. Several large, comfortable sofas to choose from, big sunny windows, rooms galore in which to lose oneself and a soft, shaggy carpet throughout. Ummm!

And, joy of joys, tucked into a corner of the garden, a large, inviting lemon tree. I Immediately went out, bowed my head and lifted a leg heavenward, thankful for the good fortune someone, somewhere had bestowed upon me.

* * * * * * *

I now live in the lap of Luxury. (Luxury is what I have named the fluffy pink bathrobe my new darling wears every morning.) I climb onto her lap and entwine myself in its warm, comforting folds as she sips her coffee and reminds her husband of all the things he forgot to do or did wrong the previous day. He just smiles and nods, obviously aware that all peace has its price. I wonder if there's a little bit of dog in him somewhere?

My days are as perfect as a dog could hope for. After the aforementioned cuddles, it's a light breakfast then off to the park where Dumb-Belle (as I affectionately think of her) chases a ball and I fossick about figuring out the mysteries of the Big Smoke. Then, home to a DentaStix and a restorative hour or three in my crate. Dumb-Belle and I each have our own but we prefer to bunk in together.

The afternoon means a walk to the lemon tree, a stretch in the sunlight and bit of a play with the cats. Yes, I have taken on the added responsibility of bringing up their two Burmese. They flick my tail, or chew my whiskers or roll about in front of me in an effort to impress. Amusing little creatures cats, if a little unsound on beef bones.

People say cats are superior creatures. Nonsense. Others are only superior if you think yourself inferior.

Evenings bring a lovely stroll around the neighbourhood, with Dumb-Belle pulling madly and me trying to restrain her.

It's taking a bit of time, but I'll get her there.

Then it's dinner, TV time on the couch with my humans and finally, bedtime. Bella climbs in first and stretches out. I crawl in after her and curl myself up in the pit of her stomach. Sometimes she'll put her head on me. Sometimes I lie between her front legs. She's warm and woolly and I lie there, safe and secure, content in the knowledge that this time, it's forever!

I wish you an equally wonderful journey!

— Beauregard of Ballarat.

Bedtime with Bella. Is there anything
as comforting as cuddling up to a Kelpie?

www.ingramcontent.com/pod-product-compliance
Lightning Source LLC
Chambersburg PA
CBHW030532020726
47494CB00004B/1325